EART
re

A Book About

The truth is incontrovertible.
Malice may attack it, ignorance may deride it,
but in the end, there it is.
Winston Churchill

There is a sufficiency in the world for man's
need, but not for man's greed.
Mahatma Gandi

SiBoRE™ - **A Simple Book Readers Edit**

Table of Contents

Author's Note . . . . page i

SiBoRE™ Defined . . . . page ii

How to Use QR Codes . . . . page iii

Chapter 1 - The Island . . . . page 1

Chapter 2 - The City . . . . page 8

Chapter 3 - The Cave . . . . page 16

Chapter 4 - The Iceberg . . . . page 23

Chapter 5 - Sea & Sky . . . . page 31

Chapter 6 - The Moon's Face . . . . page 39

Chapter 7 - Night Stars . . . . page 47

Chapter 8 - The Creature . . . . page 55

Chapter 9 - The Spirit . . . . page 67

The Plot - Poem about story . . . . page 79

About the Author . . . . page 80

ISBN 978-1-09839-880-4

Author's Note

In the book *Earth Won*, you will find references to many problems the Earth has faced in the twenty-first century of the Common Era. This story takes place in a later time period, when technology is very advanced. It is a collection of short stories written for short story products sold by E-Blox Inc. Each chapter is included in a product that offers hands-on building of objects like ships or stairs with lights. QR codes are used in this book to give educational value to the parts used to make ships or towers more than to enhance the story or plot. To allow uninterrupted reading, the eighty QR codes were moved to the end of this book on the External Links page.

Earth Won shows how brave people stand up with robots and pets against the power freaks in humanity in the future. They work together to fight an evil organization and a mysterious Creature. But the war against those who use pollution of the Earth to make a profit is challenging.

On page 79 the poem titled "The Plot" also gives an idea of what is in the story.

Art Seymour

When you will read the story, you will come across red words with an indexed reference number. In this printed book, you will find a QR code for each indexed number at the back of the book. By using a QR code reader, you will be redirected to a related internet site. These sites are dynamic and can be changed by the reader. This makes every reader of this book a potential editor!

Here's an example of how it works:

1. By using a QR code under External Links pages (81-86), you will be taken to an Internet page that is relevant to the story.
2. Now, you will have a better site that is more suitable to the story.
3. Then you follow instructions at *sibore.myeblox.com* .
4. Then your site will be accepted and you will sign an editing agreement.
5. The link from that QR code in this book will be changed by E-Blox Inc.
6. Then all future uses of that QR code will go to your new site.
7. All future uses of the normal QR99 code printed here will show your name as a *dynamic editor* and the date of edits made for that red link. Past names of dynamic editors, dates of edits made, and sites with original meanings of those editors will also appear when QR99 code is activated. All new edits will retain their meaning and purpose of clarification to the story. There is no charge for this service.

Dynamic Editors ——

qr99.myeblox.com

How to Use Quick Response (QR) Codes

To use QR codes, you must have a device with a camera that can connect to the Internet. Most cellphone cameras have this feature. There are many free QR-code readers on the Internet for all popular handheld devices. You need to focus the camera on the QR code and follow the instructions that come up on your screen: Test QR code reader here. "OK Code Reader Working" should appear.

Chapter 1
The Island

The day started like any other day as the early morning sun forced its way around the edge of the thick, lightproof shade and chased the darkness from the room. Seymour could hear the ocean waves pounding the beach in the distance as he slowly tried to pry his eyes open to wake up. Suddenly the sound of the ocean's heartbeat was broken as Robyn's soft voice announced "Good morning, sir, it is 06:32 in the morning."

Robyn had been programmed to greet people differently every morning, but this time, stamped greeting seemed to be her favorite. Seymour looked at the robot's glowing blue and green eyes and knew that she was waiting for instructions. "Good morning, Robyn,[1]" he finally said. "Would you please feed Glen while I take my shower and get dressed?"

"Yes, of course," Robyn responded as her servomotors whirred into action and she turned and glided slowly out of the bedroom. She headed toward the den where Glen[2] spent most of his night hours.

Glen

Glen was a happy, little rascal who knew that Robyn was going to give him breakfast. As soon as Robyn entered the den, the dog named Glen jumped to his feet and greeted her with three wags of his tail and a deep but friendly "woof." After less than a minute of gulping down his food and twenty licks at his water bowl, Glen ran over to the back portal that led to the beach and performed the "Glen sit." Robyn followed and transmitted a code that opened the invisible door so Glen could run out. As the fog lingered on the beach, Robyn and Glen gazed out over the mist. They could see a faint light in the distance.

Because Robyn was programmed to be curious, she instantly sent a message back to Seymour who was out of the shower and sitting at his desk, checking his morning messages. The message read, "Light at sea. Should we investigate?" The spirit of adventure grew as much as it could in a robot as Robyn's program shifted to "Scan and Protect" mode. Robyn waited for instructions. Then somewhere in the robot's top-secret receiver the answer came through: "Send Glen home and take the boat to check it out." Robyn beeped twice at Glen. The pup wagged his tail and took off for the back portal of the science lab. He was a young dog, but he always understood Robyn and did what he was told. Robyn used her boot jets to lift herself into the boat and sent a radio signal to the boat's control panel to activate the engines and set the course. The boat was well on its way as Robyn gently landed astern and on the port side[3] of the deck and started focusing on the light.

Soon an island with a building having a stairway came into focus. The light they had seen earlier was actually a red light and green light at the top of the stairway. Robyn's memory first recalled a building called the Berkeley Building in Boston[4] that used lights to forecast the weather a long time ago and then the new, more recent "Poem of the Lights."

Poem of the Lights

Both lights green, no danger seen;
Green and red, something to dread;
Both lights red, there's danger ahead.

A mystical "danger" bubble formed instantly in Robyn's unique Metatronic™ brain[5] and the boat was sent a docking command in just a millisecond. Something was moving underwater very close to the boat. The boat slowly maneuvered itself toward the pier at the bottom of the stairway in order to carry out the command, but Robyn was focused on the water, five feet off the port side, with her right arm aimed and her laser[6]—ready to fire. Then it happened: a sea creature jumped from the sea and drifted alongside the boat!

Robyn and Shadow of Sea Creature

Robyn clicked and recorded the sea creature's image in her memory, searched and compared it to over three thousand images, and had it recognized in half a second. After knowing that it was not dangerous, she lowered her laser and sent a message with the creature's image back to the lab: "I just discovered a very large spotted Hippocampus abdominalis[7] very far from home."

Then Robyn turned and watched the boat slide up against the pier and silently glide to a stop as it rubbed against the wet moss-covered planks. Even with all sensors on maximum, Robyn never saw the other figure hiding in the dark shadows under the pier. Robyn was busy sending data back to the lab. She had just transmitted the message "Location of sea creature at 54.324633, -9.637499[8]," when there was a flash of black and white fur and a single powerful leap that landed a different creature on the deck staring up at Robyn. When Robyn's mechanical structure finally caught up to the swiftness of the creature, she realized that it was a black-and-white cat that was staring at her with penetrating green eyes. The cat wore a silver collar around its neck that started beeping a message in code the instant their eyes locked on each other.

Robyn's programming allowed a little deviation when adventures produced unexpected results like this one. She instantly analyzed the feline and transmitted a message: "Devon Rex[9] encounter with an audio collar." Almost instantly the reply was received: "Her name is 'Devyn' and I need that collar. Return home." Robyn never questioned how Seymour seemed to know things with such limited data. She was programmed to be curious, but her subroutines made her a faithful companion too. Because Robyn's Metatronic™ brain allowed emotions and spiritual thoughts, you might say Robyn thought of Seymour as her father. Robyn raised her eyes slightly and said in a soft and sweet voice, "Hello Devyn."

Even though Robyn was sure that she had never met Devyn before, the collar beeped out a response in a very old form of Morse code[10]: "Hello Robyn, nice to meet you."

When Robyn and Devyn finally returned to the lab, Seymour asked Devyn to report on what she found. The data was transmitted in Morse code from Devyn's collar and both Robyn and the lab's super computer recorded the translation.

Seymour then asked Robyn to take care of Devyn and Glen by feeding them both while he looked over the data. The message was from the island, and it was very precise. Although the meaning was not totally clear, Seymour knew he would have to visit the island soon.

Morse code message

When Seymour finished, he was surprised to find that Glen and Devyn had retired to the den and were already settled in for the night.

As if Robyn could read Seymour's mind, she announced, "It's 23:18, and all are safe."

Seymour replied, "OK, thanks Robyn." Then he slowly shuffled down the hall to the sleeping chamber. After a quick electronic cleaning of his teeth and a sip of water, Seymour slid between the sheets and closed his eyes. Robyn did not need sleep and her fusion power source[11] was good for at least 80 more years. She stood in the corner, activated her long-range scan-and-protect subroutine, and waited. She could hear the heartbeats of all her biological friends in the lab, the soft rhythmic pounding of the ocean, and the gentle breeze caressing the trees nearby. She knew that she was fulfilling the purpose of her existence, and her Metatronic™ brain was at peace.

Robyn's fusion power source

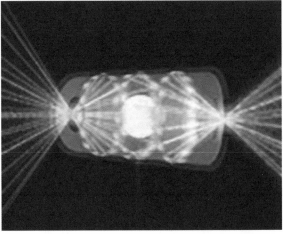

Chapter 2
The City

It was just after 2 a.m., and the city was quiet and mostly asleep. City hall, however, had one room full of activity. Even though the room had no living beings in it, at least the way most of us think of living, it was still alive with activity. Computer screens were flashing everywhere, some were showing pages of flashing data, while others were showing pictures changing so fast that they appeared to be flashing colors.

Computer screens

One screen had a drawing that looked like a flow chart[12] with areas slowly changing color or shape. The overhead lights were all off except for one, but the room was glowing green from a light source that seemed to be part of the walls. Meanwhile the power meter inside the building was recording power being used by the building. It seemed too little to support all that was taking place in this green room.

The architects of the city hall[13] saw the building as a giant sphere hanging over the River Thames. It had no front or back in conventional terms, but it derived its shape from a modified sphere, looking much like an armadillo in a protection posture.

Armadillo in a protection posture.

The activity in the room only lasted a few minutes and then everything seemed to stop. Every computer screen had a picture of a bridge, the same bridge, but viewed from different angles. The green light brightly flashed and the room suddenly returned to normal. Only one small light in the ceiling, acting as a nightlight, dimly lit the room. All the computer screens were off and all evidence of any activity disappeared.

In a lab far to the northeast, a supercomputer suddenly came alive, and on its giant screen, the pictures of the bridge from each angle appeared. There were pages of data and a strange-looking chart. One monitor showed a factory that was dumping waste into the river. A chart was blinking on and off and different chemical formulas were flashing in a small window of that screen.

Flashing data in chart

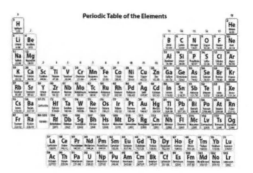

At 3 a.m., in a bedroom attached to the lab, Seymour jumped from the bed and put pressure on his left foot to bend his toes back as far as he could. A severe leg cramp had produced enough pain to make sleep impossible. He limped around the room in an attempt to get the calf of his leg normal when he noticed that his companion robot, Robyn, was not there. He limped from the sleeping chamber and down the hallway as the lab's supercomputer lit each room he was about to enter. As he passed the den, he noticed the bridge and the data displayed on the screen that took up the entire far wall.

Data Screens

The pain in his leg was instantly dismissed as he rushed back to the sleeping chamber, discarding clothes as he hustled directly through the shower tube and into the dressing area. After dressing faster than he even thought possible, he turned and saw the stairway going down to the labyrinth that existed below the sleeping chamber. The stairs were glowing green so he wasted no time descending as the floor opening above him sealed and totally isolated the lab. Robyn was waiting at the bottom of the stairway with a small briefcase that was really a remote arm of the lab's computer. Twenty feet away, sitting in an underground canal, was the top half of a small submarine-type vessel that blended into its surroundings like the mimic octopus[14], or *Thaumoctopus mimicus* as Robyn would say. Seymour called the vessel Mimi. It could change color and texture in order to blend in with the environment as well as its shape to blend with any objects it touched. The side latch to Mimi was open and a red glow came from inside. As Seymour snatched the briefcase from the robot's hand, he said, "Thanks, Robyn," and then he headed toward the open hatch. He could hear Robyn say as he entered the vessel, "Good luck, sir," and as soon as the hatch automatically closed behind him, Mimi said, "Welcome aboard, sir."

Mimi wasted no time submerging and activating the fusion-powered cavitator[15] located in her hull at the front. She soon created a pocket of air around her hull. Inside this bubble, Mimi could travel much faster without friction of water creating drag and slowing her down. Within minutes Seymour was traveling under water at almost twice the speed of sound. Because Mimi had special radar (sonar would not work at this speed) and an ability to somehow communicate with the Earth itself, the journey was quiet and smooth. During the trip, Seymour was studying the data on a display in the lid of the briefcase that was still linked to the lab's supercomputer. Due to water pollution, the footings of this very old bridge were about to give way and the bridge would almost certainly collapse.

Seymour could hear the water rush up against the hull as Mimi slowed and stopped, removing the bubble that surrounded her. Then Mimi made the hull totally transparent and the city buildings suddenly came into view. A large clock tower was the first thing that caught Seymour's eye, but there was no time for sightseeing. Seymour could see the footings of the bridge on both sides of the transparent hull and realized that he needed to act quickly. He strapped a large blue box on his back and said, "Activate." A second later, he was completely surrounded by a light-blue, transparent bubble that acted like a portable caisson[16]. The coloring made him almost invisible in the water that surrounded Mimi. Then he stepped into a small area near the hatch and seemed to walk right through the hull and onto the sandy bottom near one of the bridge's footings. As soon as he touched the footing, the bubble expanded and surrounded the entire damaged area with an intelligence that seemed to come from nowhere. Seymour knew that the box on his back, the computer in his lab, and the Earth itself were all controlling the repair. The footings seemed to be damaged by bacterial corrosion and calcium leaching[17]. The source of the damaging stimuli that produced these effects in the exposed concrete on the footings would need to be stopped.

It only took a few minutes at each footing and Seymour was back inside Mimi before 5 a.m. The city was starting to come to life, but Seymour knew that he had more work ahead as he softly said, "Park me near the bridge please, Mimi." In a few minutes, the small submarine moved parallel to the brick walkway that followed the water and transformed to look like an old pier that was barely visible to any pedestrians that might pass.

Under the bridge, where no camera or person could view, Seymour came magically through the holographic pier boards and started walking to a ladder that led to the walkway. Once on the walkway, he found himself standing in front of an old structure built between 1087 and 1100 by Edward the Confessor[18]. He recognized it because it was one of the largest medieval halls still in existence. It had always fascinated Seymour because at one time it had an unsupported hammerbeam roof. After a fire, it was rebuilt and became a landmark with the clock tower that chimes on the hour. He walked directly toward the entrance of the building. It was still very early and only a few people were there on the walkway.

Clock tower and walkway

Seymour entered the building with the briefcase from the lab hanging from his left hand. He looked like any other businessman dealing with the decision makers who would soon be arriving. He proceeded directly to an overnight mail slot located next to a locked door. On the glass in the door only three letters were printed—GLA, which stood for the Greater London Authority oversight committee. A sealed envelope slowly ejected from the side of his briefcase into his right hand. He dropped it through the slot, left the building, and was back inside Mimi in a matter of minutes.

Mimi then returned him back to his sleeping chamber. A few hours later, the GLA,[19] which was responsible for the strategic administration of the entire city, was buzzing like a fallen hornet's nest. Multiple reports of industrial pollution with data and charts had somehow been discovered. There was a nearby factory located on the Thames that was seriously highlighted in the report. Even the Mayor and Crime division were involved investigating the pollution source.

Seymour slipped between the warm sheets and said, "Just a couple hours, Robyn." His faithful companion stood motionless in the corner of the sleeping chamber and responded in a soft sweet voice, "Yes sir." The chamber was not very dark, but sleep was taking over fast as Seymour thought, *"Another adventure was over ... or was it?"*

Chapter 3
The Cave

After a long day of climbing the mountain on the island, Seymour's stomach and legs were telling him that it was time to rest and get something to eat. From the position of the sun, he knew that it was late in the afternoon and began to worry a little about his situation. The instructions he had received from Devyn's collar told him to take nothing but a light source, water, and climbing tools[20] with him. However, now that hunger was starting to make an appearance in this latest adventure, while trust was starting to make a retreat, he sat on a chair-size rock to give his legs a break and took a sip from his waterskin.[21]

A cloud passed overhead and blotted out the sun for a few seconds, and then he saw the dim light glowing from a crack in the mountainside in the distance. Since Earth had communicated with him like this before, Seymour knew that the cloud was no coincidence, and the ache in his legs suddenly vanished. He jumped to his feet and started making his way toward the area where he noticed a dim light. The cloud was gone and took the dim glow with it. Only Seymour's faith in what he saw motivated him now. Seymour knew faith without action meant nothing!

It was a very difficult spot on the face of the mountain, and it took almost an hour to reach the narrow crack located on a nearly vertical wall of the mountain. He was almost out of pitons[22] when he reached the crack that was only a few inches wide.

Piton anchor

Darkness had nearly settled in and Seymour felt fear for the first time. What was he doing on the side of a mountain just to look into a crack? He almost fell when he placed his hand in the crack to pull himself closer, but instead the rock slid back to make a doorway that allowed him inside. Seymour steadied himself and entered the hidden cave. The floor of the cave was smooth and flat, and as he stepped forward, the door to the cave completely closed behind him and all light vanished. He unclipped the light source from his belt and turned it on. He said to himself, *"Now I know why I was told to bring a light source. Thank God that I brought the best one I could find."* He knew the batteries in this lamp could last for days and it was smart enough to adjust to the environment.

The sensors in the light source set the lamp's intensity, then the microchip[23] changed the color for best viewing. It was the same shade of light that the crack displayed when the cloud passed over. Seymour's eyes slowly adjusted to the new conditions and the cave walls came into focus. There were two symbols carved into the rock on each side of the cave. The first one looked like an umbrella with a fat, straight handle followed by an arrow pointing to a downward passage. The opposite wall had a symbol that looked like a triangle and was followed by an arrow that pointed to an upward path in the cave.

Wall carving

Just then, Seymour's stomach growled for food loud enough to produce an echo in the cave. He decided to move on the downward path and started cautiously and slowly into that passage. As he made his way down, the walls displayed strange carvings. One of them reminded him of an ancient mammal that he had studied in school, called the Mastodon.[24] He recalled, as he slowly moved down the path, how much fun it was to discover facts from the past that helped to form this world of today. The cave path slowly turned to the left and opened into a large underground chamber. He could hear the sound of water running, and the air grew heavy and moist. His lamp automatically adjusted to a brighter setting and he could see that the chamber was as large as a sports stadium and had a small pool of water on the far side. There were at least three other openings that he could see in the walls of the chamber, and he felt like a cave explorer who was going spelunking.[25]

Seymour's stomach once again demanded attention, so he decided to head over toward the pool to see if there was anything edible. When he reached the side of the pool, he found a good-sized field of mushrooms and realized that the umbrella-shaped carving was a signpost to this spot. He sat on a rock at the edge of the mushroom garden and pondered his fate. There were no footprints in the dust around the mushrooms. Then again, there were no bones to be seen either. There was only one thing he could trust now. He flipped off his lamp and the chamber went totally dark. He waited as the pupils of his eyes dilated to let in more light. Nothing! Minutes went by and still nothing. Seymour's faith was strong and he trusted that the Earth would give him a sign. He could hear the trickle of water running into the pool nearby, but he could see nothing. He felt a slight breeze on his right arm like someone had just walked past him and the hair on his neck uncurled. He slowly glanced in that direction and there it was, a small patch of Shimeji[26] mushrooms with a dim color-changing glow.

Seymour flipped the lamp back on and ate without fear. He knew Earth would not give him anything harmful. He remembered those days when he was very young and his grandmother would give him strange things to eat, but always with a smile and great love in her heart. He felt that same love coming from Earth as he took his first bite of the mushroom. It was chewy and slightly sweet. He thought it sort of tasted like the homemade licorice candy[27] that his grandmother made when he was young. He ate his fill and started looking for a place to sit. Finding a mossy flat spot near the wall of the cavern, Seymour sat with his back resting against the wall and recorded the day's events in his notebook. When all was faithfully documented, he put away his notes and enjoyed the beauty of this underground world.

How lucky he was for even inside the belly of a mountain, Earth was like a loving grandmother—old, majestic, and beautiful. Even the pilea cavernicola[28]

Pilea flowers

flowers that surrounded him seemed to be planted by his grandmother. He flipped off the lamp and used his arm as a pillow as he laid down on the hard moss mattress. He felt more like he was in the bed in his grandmother's attic with all the love that surrounded him in those days and drifted off into a peaceful sleep.

During the night, Seymour dreamed. It was not a normal, vague type of dream, but a lucid dream with vivid images and fantastic colors. He could see the cave as it was before man walked the Earth. There were animals on the planet then, and a few presented themselves to Seymour in a manner that did not feel like a dream. It was more like a tour through a holographic museum. And there were sounds in the dream—yes, the actual sounds of these strange creatures. He had never seen some of them before; others were more familiar because their bones were discovered and put into museums that he had visited on school trips when he was young. He recognized a T-Rex[29] that stared into his eyes and roared to show how ferocious he once was. Still this once-mighty animal was subject to Earth and its ever-changing climate. The T-Rex with all its majesty, brought a flavor of sadness into the dream—a taste that would stay with Seymour for many years to come.

Then suddenly, Seymour opened his eyes and found that the chamber was full of light. The sun that always retires in the west had risen in the east and found many tiny cracks at the top of the cavern that illuminated this underground world like a thousand stadium laser lights. With the dream still fresh in his mind, he sat up, grabbed his notebook and pen, and started recording everything he could remember from it. He made sketches of every animal in his nightly adventure that was new to him and wished he had a way to add the color, but that would have to be done when he got back to the lab. He also remembered the sky from his dream. It was strangely scary and filled with foreboding. "Perhaps," he wrote in his notes, "it was a clue to the extinction[30] of these creatures that lived over 60 million years ago."

He knew the two theories, but now he was convinced that it was not the meteor from another world theory, but the Earth itself that had changed everything in preparation to the existence of man on the planet. His newfound belief supported the volcano theory and just made more sense. But then, not everyone was as closely connected to Earth as Seymour.

He was anxious to get home and record his dream in the supercomputer. He also wanted to search for data about the animals that appeared to him in his dream and were new to him. He trusted his connection with Earth and followed a path that led him straight to a hidden underground river that flowed swiftly into the ocean, about ten feet below the surface at low tide. He could see the light from the ocean as he stared down into the river. He knew that he would be safe, so he dove into the river toward the light and was swiftly pushed down by the current and out into the ocean. He realized that the current was too swift to swim against and the only way back would be another tough climb to the hidden door. He also knew that his submarine, Mimi, could bring him back to the cave. It was almost noon when he finally got back to the lab. He was home again, but this time he knew that there was another place that could be a home to him, too—the cave.

Chapter 4
The Iceberg

Warning sirens were sounding all over the ship as the Research Vessel, the Thomas G Thompson,[31] received an SOS and Mayday from the science bio-copter that fluttered into sight. Like a large dragonfly, the out-of-control bio-copter banged onto the deck and slid into a cargo area. The four transparent wings disappeared into the side of the copter and its invisible shields were removed so Seymour could jump from the cockpit and stagger onto the deck. The emergency crew ran toward the copter with fire fighters ready to put out any fire, as Seymour raised his hands and shouted, "It's OK, I just had a fuel cell fail and lost power in the main tri-blade. There's no threat of fire." When he explained that he was on his way to investigate a sighting of an unusual Iceberg, the captain welcomed him aboard and stated they were on the same mission.

Thomas G. Thompson Research Vessel

Seymour accepted the invitation to join the crew and scientists who were already aboard and travel with them to the last-transmitted sighting of the iceberg. It was an old ship, but the vessel could still berth up to thirty-six scientific personnel, twenty-one officers, crew, and two technicians.

Seymour had been away from home for almost a week now, and his eyes longed to see Robyn floating around the lab. His hands wanted to reach down and pet Glen. He longed for the lab and all of its blinking lights and familiar humming sounds. He was homesick and wondered why he felt it was important that he take this trip on the Ocean Research Vessel. Like many of his adventures before, he just knew that he had to be on this ship at this time. A blast from the whooper alarm and people running toward the bow snapped him back to reality as he joined the scramble to the front of the ship. The smell of ozone was strong even though the wind had increased significantly. The ship was being tossed from side to side as the waves were now coming from every direction. Just as the rain started, Seymour caught a glimpse of people pointing at a shiny iceberg[32] in the center of the approaching storm. He also felt TB, Seymour's Tri-Blade (TB) bio-copter, directly above him with shields at maximum and a rope ladder swishing all around him.

He was having difficulty climbing when suddenly the ladder stiffened as though someone was holding the loose end. Looking down he noticed that someone with a large backpack was on the ladder behind him and was climbing toward him. He quickly scurried to the top, entered the copter, and turned to help his pursuer through the door as the bio-copter jerked forward and threw them both up against the back wall. Seymour had little time to study his new companion with the large backpack, wearing a bright-yellow hooded rain jacket that only exposed a small portion of his face, but he looked young and eager to get to work. Then the copter landed on the iceberg with such force that both of the copters' passengers bounced forward.

The storm seemed to vanish as the shield from the bio-copter expanded to cover the entire iceberg. Seymour knew exactly what needed to be done as he pulled a lever at the top of the cockpit and released TB. Tri-Blade jumped from the bio-copter and fastened itself to the tip of the iceberg, which appeared to be made of glass once the rain and waves were removed by the invisible shield that eliminated the storm's fury. For a moment Seymour had forgotten about his uninvited passenger who seemed to be a very young boy. Because Seymour was watching TB and had his vision focused on the tip of the iceberg, he failed to notice that his new companion had jumped from the copter and removed four red-brick-like objects from his backpack. He was attaching them at the point where the water met the "glassberg" with a laser ray from a strange-looking welding[33] tool. He worked with incredible speed and had finished attaching the fourth and last red brick when Seymour suddenly realized that the young man was also in touch with the spirit of the Earth and was performing without question what he knew must be done. Snapping back to reality, Seymour opened the cockpit door of the bio-copter and reached out to grasp the hand of his new companion just as the shield collapsed and the ferocity of the storm returned. His new friend was almost sucked into the hurricane-level winds and it took both hands with feet braced against both sides of the doorframe to pull him into the cockpit. Seymour slammed the door and the roar of the hurricane outside was reduced significantly.

The Thomas G. Thompson Research Vessel could no longer see the iceberg due to the heavy rain and waves that tossed the vessel around like a ping-pong ball in a shower stall.

Then suddenly the storm stopped. The waves were gone and so was the iceberg. In the sky, using clouds for cover, a huge triangular object was moving north at incredible speed. It was surrounded by an electromagnetic field[34] that bent electronic waves and made them undetectable by any existing radar. Inside the body of the bio-copter that was attached to the flying triangle, Seymour's new companion had just untied the string on the hood of his raincoat and pulled the hood down. Long beautiful red hair fell to cover the shoulders of the most beautiful woman Seymour had ever seen. She turned and looked into Seymour's eyes and spoke for the first time. "Wow! That was fun," she said.

Seymour stared at her with his mouth open, looking like a carp in a fish bowl, and he said, "You're a girl!"

She laughed at his comment as she pulled off the rest of her raincoat and then extended her hand and said, "Hi. I'm Ruby."

Seymour's shock seemed to disappear as he closed his mouth, reached to take her hand, and said "Hi, I'm Seymour."

Their hands engaged and the universe evolved to a new level. A moment in time that will never be recorded in any book, but will be forever part of the earth's history. Like two soap bubbles touching in space and gently becoming united, two souls amplified each other by an order of magnitude and many mysteries of the Earth were revealed. They increased their grasp, stared into each other's eyes with wonder, and both had an epiphany. It was a moment of great and sudden revelation.

They knew that the great triangle they were riding on was made of pure carbon. It was a diamond the size of a mountain! They knew that a group of giant isopod[35] living at extremely high pressure on the ocean floor had taken carbon dioxide from the ocean and created this pure carbon diamond while releasing oxygen into the air. They knew the Earth was using a group of creatures in a new way to lower the carbon footprint man was creating. And they knew they were now two of the most advanced creatures in this group.

Giant isopod

During the trip, Seymour and Ruby shared the many adventures they had been on that were similar to the one they were on now. Seymour explained how he found TB when he was very young and Ruby explained her discovery of the four red antimatter[36] bricks. They knew now that they both were required to perform this task and understood why the diamond needed to remain a secret. If the diamond industry discovered this secret, its impact on the global economic market would be devastating.

Their discussion was interrupted by the descent and reduction in speed. They both suspected that this diamond would be placed on a high plateau[37] on an island near Seymour's lab. It would be covered by earth and rocks and appear to be just another small mountain peak. As they watched, their suspicions were made reality by TB, the anti-matter bricks, and the spirit of the Earth that guided the mission.

After replacing TB on the bio-copter and disconnecting all the antimatter bricks, Seymour and Ruby returned to the bio-copter and flew to the beach near Seymour's lab. A blue light was glowing from the lab window and Seymour knew it was time to leave Ruby in the hands of TB. As he exited the copter, he gave her hand one last squeeze, and, without speaking, they both knew they would work together again. Seymour entered the lab through a hidden portal that opened just as the bio-copter whooshed off the beach. The first to greet him was Glen, the little dog he loved so much. Then Robyn, his companion robot, floated into the room and said, "Welcome back, sir."

Seymour hesitated and stared at Robyn for a moment. Robyn's voice was always very feminine, but now it had a familiar ring to it. He finally answered back and said, "Thank you, Robyn. I'm really glad to be back."

Robyn took a 180 degree turn and led Seymour out of the room and down the hall. While leaving she remarked, "Food has been prepared if you are hungry." There was no denying it; there was something in Robyn's voice that made him think of Ruby.

Later that night, after TB and the bio-copter had delivered Ruby to her home far away, her faithful robot companion, Max, greeted her as she entered the house with "Welcome back, miss." Ruby hesitated and stared at Max for a moment. Max's voice was always very masculine but gentle, and now it had a familiar ring to it.

She finally answered back, "Thank you, Max. I'm really happy to be back." Max took a 180 degree turn and led Ruby out of the room and into the eating area. While leaving he remarked, "Food has been prepared if you are hungry." There was no denying it; there was something in Max's voice that made her think of Seymour.

That night many storms around the globe ended, all but one at the top of a mountain near Seymour's lab. And as Seymour watched it through his sleeping-chamber window while he lied in bed, he knew the Earth was at work, protecting its children. He closed his eyes and slipped into a peaceful sleep.

Chapter 5
Sea & Sky

Seymour was dreaming of those days long ago, when he was only 14 and had spotted something glowing in the water. It had been hot that summer, and Seymour was looking for an adventure when he walked barefoot down to the bayou[38] to cool his feet. The water level was extremely low due to lack of rain, lower than he had ever seen it before. There it was, a curved wing of a helicopter blade with a blue glow sticking out of the muck on the other side. The dream was vivid with all the details of how it took him and his father two days to pull it from the muck and drag it back to the farm. Suddenly he was awake with all the dream details poking at his brain. Robyn sensed something was different and replaced her usual greeting with "Is everything alright, sir?"

Seymour responded, "I'm not sure, Robyn, but I think TB is trying to tell me something." Robyn knew that TB was the Tri-Blade that her friend communicated with long before she met him, so she waited for further instructions. "Robyn, please take care of the lab while I get a cup of coffee and think about my discovery of TB for a while." Robyn knew that no response was required and went about completing the request while the supercomputer[39] that ran the lab was already pouring a cup of coffee in the kitchen.

Seymour sat at the counter, took his first sip of coffee, and let his mind drift back to the day when he, with his father, had first launched TB. Seymour just took his last sip of coffee when he heard the whooshing sound of TB landing on the beach near the lab. He knew the dream last night was not a random event, but a communication from TB and was anxious to find out what was so important.

32

Seymour smiled as he put the cup on the counter because he knew it would be cleaned and back in the processor before he returned. He quickly went back to the sleeping area, walked through the shower chamber, and dressed for a trip outside.

As he walked toward the wall at the far side of the sleeping chamber, the lab's supercomputer seemed to sense his intentions and opened a hidden portal to the beach. He hurried toward the bio-copter[40] that used TB as a lifting source instead of wings that were hidden in its sides, and the portal closed behind him. The cockpit's pure blue light got brighter as TB removed the invisible shield to allow entry. Seymour knew that TB was really controlling the bio-copter, but then only he knew the real power of TB. Like many of the miracles on Earth, TB was connected to the lab's supercomputer by millions of invisible pathways that surrounded everything. Every molecule was used by the Earth to connect, transmit, and unite the structures and creatures like nerves in a living organism. Very few understood this connection or how to use it. Seymour was the one who understood it best, as he let TB force the bio-copter to cut through the sky at a speed near to that of sound. The sky ahead appeared to be changing to a deeper shade of blue as Seymour stared through the cockpit windshield and wondered what the emergency was. His mind drifted back to the first trip with TB in control. He was just a teenager and was using TB to push his homemade swamp boat[41] up the bayou toward the Kankakee River. As he continued to reminisce about this first trip with TB, he recalled that suddenly TB seemed to have a mind of its own as it turned the vessel pushing it through the cattails and into the tall grass of the swampland.

TB controlling swamp boat

Seymour tried to turn back, but he could not turn the boat and then it just stopped right next to a large fourteen-point male deer that was stuck in the vines and muck. Without thinking, he made a loop in the end of the boat's docking rope and threw it over the horns of the exhausted animal. The imperial stag[42] turned and stared at TB and the animal's eyes seemed to turn blue. Tri-Blade suddenly came to life and Seymour was thrown back and forth in the boat. Tri-Blade and stag seemed to work in unison until the stag was free. Then TB stopped, and the blue glow left the stag's eyes as he lumbered through the water toward the edge of the forest, where a doe and fawn were cautiously watching. After this rescue, Seymour always thought of TB by the name TB because he realized it had an intelligent nature and was much more than just a propeller.

Stag after freedom from killing vine

The journey was getting turbulent and it shook Seymour out of his daydreaming. TB slowed the bio-copter and dropped down to about one hundred feet above the ocean surface. The water below was bubbling furiously and the gas released[43] into the air made it feel like the bio-copter was in a violent storm. The cockpit light turned bright blue and Seymour knew that this was where TB needed to be. As they flew south and slowly away from the boiling ocean, a ship came into view. It was a cruise ship, very large with many women and children on the deck. TB wasted no time and landed the bio-copter on the copter-pad near the bridge. TB shut down, dropped the shields, and turned the cockpit's blue light off. At the same time, the bridge lights turned bright blue and reminded Seymour of the stag's eyes those many years ago. Knowing what TB was doing, he jumped from the cockpit and ran toward the bridge.

All the people on the bridge were staring up at the lights and wondering why they were blue. The captain of the ship jumped as Seymour burst onto the bridge and shouted, "Stop the ship! Now! Full astern[44]! Deadly waters ahead!" The lights on the bridge turned deeper blue as Seymour yelled, "Hurry!" The captain, unwilling to be the cause of a disaster, repeated the orders and the ship suddenly lurched to a stop and started moving away from the bubbling ocean that could now be easily seen dead ahead.

Deck chairs slid forward and passengers staggered on the deck. A couple of books fell off the shelf on the bridge, but no serious damage was reported. Everyone started calling the bridge to ask what happened, and for the next few minutes, the captain was very busy telling them that everything was all right. He kept saying to each caller: "I will fill you in later." Finally, the phone lights stopped blinking and the captain turned to Seymour and asked, "What's going on?"

Seymour explained how gas from the ocean floor was being rapidly released and how it lowered the density of the water. The large ship could not be supported in this low-density water and would have plunged to the ocean floor. Just then the bridge lights and the bridge returned to normal.

"What's going on with these lights?" asked the captain. "And how did you do that?"

Seymour replied, "It means you're safe now. Just keep away from that swirling, bubbling water, and everything will be OK."

Bermuda Triangle waters

After Seymour reply, he noticed that TB had turned the light of bio-copter's cockpit blue. "I've got to go now" was his response to the second question, and Seymour hurried off the bridge and back to the bio-copter that seemed to be powering up on its own. Before he was even inside, TB lifted them off the platform and headed back toward the lab. There was a message beeping in Morse code on the headset as Seymour placed it around his neck and let the speakers hang down near his chest. He knew it was TB transmitting back to the lab the coordinates of the hot spot that he was sure was in the triangle[45] and asking Robyn to get a warning out to all the ships in the area. Knowing that it would be late by the time they returned to the lab, Seymour tried to close his eyes and get some sleep. There were many memories running through his mind about all the rescues he and TB had made together. This was just like all of the rest—do what is needed to be done and quickly disappear. It was strange how TB seemed to talk to him without using any words or language. Was it telepathy[46] with the planet? He felt more connected to the Earth through TB on each rescue. TB was surely part of it, but somehow there was something greater happening. As home and the lab came into view, he could feel the lab calling him. It was as if it was saying, "Welcome back."

Then he heard again, that faint clicking sound, coming from nowhere and everywhere at the same time. He pulled his notebook out of his pocket and tried to record the sound that was much like a distant rattling. He knew it was a message from Earth, but how do you write down a rattling sound? TB dropped Seymour on the beach near the lab and waited until he was safely inside before lifting the bio-copter to the hanger high on the nearby island mountaintop. Seymour heard TB's departure from inside the lab and sent a mental message, "Good night, TB." Although there was no real response, he could feel TB answering, "Good night, my friend." Then he asked Robyn if Glen was asleep, and she told him that he was not back from his latest adventure. Glen often disappeared for a few days, but he always found his way back—so Seymour did not worry.

Seymour tried to record all the events of the day in his computer logs while he ate a sandwich and drank the hot chocolate that Robyn had made for him. Soon the day's adventure demanded rest and Robyn helped Seymour to have a shower and go to bed. The last thing he heard as his mind surrendered control was Robyn's sweet voice saying, "Good night." It made him think of Ruby, and he knew that he was about to have a beautiful dream.

Robyn

Chapter 6
The Moon's Face

It was one of those nights when the sky becomes a picture to remember in the Earth's museum of art. Seymour was lying in bed with his hands behind his head and fingers interlocked. He was staring at the moon through the one-way skylight in his sleeping chamber as clouds slowly strolled through the scene. He was thinking how the face[47] on the moon always looked like someone with one eye closed trying to get a better look at the Earth. Suddenly the face changed! The other eye opened and both eyes turned bright red. Seymour thought that he must be dreaming, so he sat up, rubbed his eyes, and stared back at the moon again. Both red eyes staring back at him were still there. Robyn glided into the room holding a wet suit with diving belt and a special backpack. Her Metatronic™ brain seemed to know things that needed to be done, and Seymour trusted her more than anyone else he knew. He climbed into the suit, and as he struggled to secure the backpack, he asked, "Do you know where I'm going?"

"Our MCT[48] has failed, and the lab is running on auxiliary power," she explained. Then she added, "I will need to stay here in case backup fails. If it does, I will switch the lab over to my fusion power source until you get the Turbine fixed."

Seymour strapped on the diving belt as he walked toward the back wall of the sleeping chamber. He stopped short when the invisible portal did not open.

"You will have to use the side door," Robyn said matter of factly. "All unnecessary power is on hold." She then led Seymour out of the sleeping chamber and down the hall to the seldom-used mechanical door that led to the beach. Two red lights were showing that the door was now unlocked and ready to be used. Robyn opened the emergency door and Seymour carefully stepped down onto the beach.

As Robyn closed the door behind him, he touched a small patch on the backpack strap and said, "Activate!" A blue bubble of air, captivated by a force field shield and holographic display appeared. He heard Robyn say, "Good luck, sir." and knew that the communications link was working and she would be monitoring the task ahead. He quickly jogged into the ocean pausing only slightly as each wave was split by his wet suit. His progress slowed as he submerged and the force-field air bubble displaced enough water to make him start to rise to the surface. The microcircuit in the backpack immediately adjusted the size of the breathing bubble to make Seymour perfectly buoyant, like a submersible[49] going to zero bubble. Then two small jets on each side of the backpack engaged and he was propelled forward at significant speed. He heard Robyn's voice proclaim, "You will be at the site in 12 minutes and 18 seconds."

He knew that the Earth and the moon, somehow through Robyn, were now in control. His body was adjusted to a slight downward angle to keep him close to the ocean floor as his speed gradually increased. With depth came darkness, but his backpack lit up and cast two red beams of light to show what was ahead. Then it came into view just as Seymour noticed a decrease in speed. From the ocean's surface it looked like a large coral reef, but from his view, it was a giant structure that funneled ocean's water into the turbine. The structure used Bernoulli's Principle[50] to accelerate the tidal flow that passed through the turbine, generating electrical power for Seymour's home and laboratory. There was a grid in front of the tunnel that led to the turbine designed to keep fish and debris away from the blade. The backpack, guided by Robyn from the lab, put Seymour safely on the side of the rushing waters going through the angled grid that pushed the fish to the side but let the water rush through. As his feet touched the ocean floor, he heard Robyn say, "You are in control now."

Similar underwater turbine

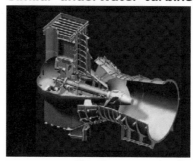

The holographic display led him to a maze around the grid and away from the water, rushing through the enormous turbine blade. The blade was spinning five times faster than normal and Seymour could feel a vibration getting stronger. He knew that there was no time to waste as he moved quickly toward a three-foot control wheel that was diverting the water away from the blade before it cracked or exploded. Turning the wheel clockwise forced a titanium plate to slide in front of the blade and at the same time open a new path for the water. The vibration slowed and finally disappeared when the plate totally covered the blade. Two red lights came on showing a passage to a chamber door.

Seymour never considered himself as a hero, but the rapid pounding of his heart as the vibration stopped told him fear abounded. He was afraid he might not survive! There was a connection, however, with Earth itself that drove him to do these things without question. Then there was Robyn, who always kept him on track, and her voice filled his bubble of air, "The lab is at twenty percent reserve, and I am connecting my power source to slow down the drain on the batteries. Please hurry." He knew that her Metatronic™ brain would make her sacrifice herself to save the lab, and that was not an acceptable scenario.

Pulling a lever on the chamber door allowed seawater to fill the interlock and turned the two lights a dim yellow. He entered the interlock that operated like a torpedo tube[51] chamber in reverse, closed the door, and reset the lever from inside. The seawater quickly drained through a grate in the floor and the lights turned green. A panel on the wall opposite the seawater door slid open and Seymour entered the well-lit generator room as he touched the strap on his chest and removed the air bubble surrounding his head. The smell of hot steel filled the room, but no fire or smoke could be seen. The Generator Repair Robot (GR2) was motionless and standing by the blade shaft with something in its claw. GR2 was a highly advanced industrial robot.[52] Upon further inspection, Seymour discovered that a gear had exploded and a piece must have pierced GR2's power source. GR2 had pulled it free, but the robot's power ran out before it could do anything else.

The missing gear allowed the blade to spin freely and overheat a bearing on the shaft that was no longer connected to the generator. Pulling a spare power source from storage, Seymour first repaired GR2 and told him to get the bearing replaced. In his earpiece, he heard Robyn's voice reporting, "Down to fifteen percent energy level." He knew that he had to get the generator back on line soon. There were no spare gears in the storage area and he was at a loss on what to do next. Then it happened! Seymour felt a small breeze, as if someone had just passed him. There was no one else in the room and goose bumps made the hairs on his arm stand up as he felt it again. A small whirlwind of air had formed in the corner of the room and revealed three shapes of gears in the clay floor that had been covered and filled with years of dust and dirt. GR2 was still working on the bearing on the other side of the room and there was no visible source for this mini tornado. Then it moved and hovered over a pile of steel pellets lying on the floor for a few seconds and disappeared.

Small Whirlwind

Seymour moved swiftly as he placed some of the pellets in the clay mold of the correct-sized gear and pulled a laser welder down from the shelf. He attached a cable from the backpack to the laser to give it maximum power, set the dial on heat, placed it about six inches over the pellets, and pulled the trigger. The steel turned cherry red, then white hot, then started to act like a fourth of July sparkler, and finally melted. His backpack beeped, letting him know that the energy level was extremely low, so he released the trigger on the laser. He added a few more pellets to fill the mold and thicken the gear and watched as they slowly melted and became part of the pool of liquid steel. GR2 suddenly appeared at his side and started spraying the new gear with a fire extinguisher to rapidly cool down the gear and set the temper.[53] They worked as a team now to replace the gear and finish the repairs. Just as they finished, he heard Robyn's voice announce, "Energy level at ten percent." Pressing the patch on the backpack strap, he activated the air bubble as he entered the interlock. Water quickly filled the interlock, but the air bubble was flashing a red light indicating that there was less than one minute of energy left in the backpack.

He reached the gate wheel and started to turn it just when the bubble turned solid red and he knew this was it. He took a long last breath of air as the bubble vanished and the sea slapped his face. He finished turning the wheel until the gate was fully opened then started making his way through the maze and back to the open ocean. He knew he could never remove the backpack or weights in time to make it to the surface. His lungs were already starting to burn, as they desired a fresh supply of air. Then he heard it again, that clicking sound that he had heard before on other missions. After stumbling from the maze and into the ocean, he stood straight in the dark to hear where the sound was coming from. Two dolphins[54] appeared from behind him, placed themselves on each side, and lifted him to the surface by pressing against him quickly.

Seymour remembered the wonderful feel of the fresh air as his head broke the surface. He remembered how the two dolphins clicked the same pattern of sounds as they swiftly took him to Robyn standing in waste-high water, waiting to carry him into the sleeping chamber. Removing his backpack and wet suit and getting into bed was just a blur. He remembers staring at the moon one last time before he closed his eyes. The moon's face was normal and even seemed to be smiling. But what he remembers the most before he drifted away was the song the dolphins sang as they brought him to Robyn. He had heard the rhythm of those clicks before and wanted to know what it meant. Like a lullaby, it put him to sleep.

That night he dreamed about Ruby. Perhaps it was hearing Robyn's voice before he hit the pillow that made him dream of her, but his dreams always meant something. He pictured her as a princess in a castle with servants and loyal subjects who lived all around her. The dream seemed real, and they were getting married in it. When dawn came, he did not want to open his eyes. He did not want the dream to stop. Then he thought it was just a silly dream ... or was it?

Seymours Dream

Chapter 7
Night Stars

Ruby was not aware of the drop in temperature as she continued to stare at the stars from her mountaintop bench. It was just a short walk back to her palace chamber, but she was mesmerized by the clarity of the night stars. Max, her robotic companion, floated in quietly behind her and gently placed a soft thick blanket over her shoulders and back to eliminate exposure to the cold. Ruby welcomed the blanket but never took her eyes off the sky as she pulled the blanket around her and remarked, "I can see them all so clear, Max." Then jumping from the bench and pointing at a spot in the sky, Ruby, filled with excitement, yelled, "Look! Look at Delphinus[55]! Can you see it?" Although Max had a Metatronic™ brain, he was not always capable of seeing like some of the gifted humans he had met. He knew the constellation of stars that was called Delphinus or the Dolphin, but that was all he saw—a cluster of stars. He responded with his unemotional and deep masculine voice, "Yes miss, I see it."

Ruby's Vision

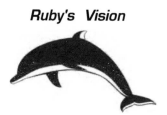

Ruby knew that he was only seeing the stars, and not the Dolphin. She knew that this was either a message from the past or a prophesy. She picked up the blanket that had fallen to the ground, wrapped it around her, slowly sat back on the bench, and said quietly, *"I wonder what it means?"* Ruby recalled from Greek mythology the story about a Greek poet, Arion of Lesbos, who was saved by a dolphin. She wondered if this sign was for her or, perhaps, someone she knew. She rose from the bench and followed Max back to the palace built inside the mountain. He was a faithful companion that seemed to know what she was thinking most of the time, but this time he could not help her.

Meanwhile, far away in another land, Seymour sat looking at the night sky from a flat rock on the beach near his laboratory home. He was not aware of the drop in temperature as he continued to stare at the stars from his favorite resting place. It was just a short walk back to the laboratory, but he was mesmerized by the clarity of the night stars. Robyn, his robotic companion, floated in quietly next to him and placed a soft thick blanket over his shoulders and back to eliminate exposure to the cold sea breeze. Seymour welcomed the blanket, but he never took his eyes off the sky as he remarked, "I feel the stars have something to tell me, Robyn." Pointing he exclaimed, "Look at that grouping over there, Robyn. It's so bright and red!" Robyn responded sweetly in a soft whisper, "It almost looks like a ruby." Then she turned and floated slowly back toward the lab. Seymour stayed for a while, wondering what it all meant. He remembered his adventure where he had met Ruby and how much he had enjoyed their conversation and time together. Another constellation caught his attention before he left the beach. Suddenly an arrow seemed to shoot across the sky. It was from a bow in the star cluster known as Orion[56] the hunter.

Ruby's galaxy

The next morning Seymour was awakened by the clicking of dolphins on the beach. It was not a gentle sound, but harsh and shrill, almost like a call for help. Robyn entered the room with a tray that supported the smallest breakfast he had ever seen. Robyn stated, "Please eat quickly, sir, there is an emergency at the beach." Seymour gobbled down a piece of toast as he slipped into the wet suit that Robyn had previously laid on the chair by his bed. He flushed his throat out with half a glass of orange juice and slipped the power pack on his back without comment. No need to ask, he knew Robyn would fill him in before he hit the beach. The portal in the sleeping chamber wall that led to the beach opened, and as he rose to walk through it, Robyn said, "They need your help." She handed him a waterproof medical case called the MedTab[57] as he stepped onto the beach and tapped the switch on the power-pack strap to activate the air bubble, camera, and holographic screen. When Seymour reached the water, he noticed two large dolphins swimming in a circle around a small baby dolphin. The calf was motionless and floating on one side. An arrow from a speargun was protruding from both sides of the calf's dorsal ridge a few inches behind the dorsal fin. Seymour steadied himself and aimed the MedTab camera at the calf. And within seconds an x-ray[58] image of the calf appeared on his holographic screen at the front of his air bubble helmet. He thought that he heard Robyn speaking behind him, but when he turned, he saw Ruby in a wet suit, similar to his, holding a red, antigravity brick. She placed the brick under the calf, lifted him out of the water, and they both rushed toward the lab's operating room where Robyn and Max were ready to take over. Max looked at Seymour and said, "Hello, I'm Ruby's companion, Max" and then began working with Robyn to save the calf. Seymour had never met Max, but his voice could have made him Seymour's twin brother.

X-ray of baby dolphin

With the aid of the lab's computer, Robyn and Max removed the speargun arrow and sealed the wound quickly. The calf was weak, but it was resting normally as they gently lowered him into the warm recovery tank in the lab floor that was often used by Seymour as a spa pool. The only difference now was an AC current[60] flowing through the water in the pool to aid the healing process. As the frequency of the current changed, the light in the wall of the tank would change color, indicating about the calf's recovery. When they knew that the calf was going to be OK, Seymour and Ruby went down to the beach to assure the other dolphins that the danger was past. Somehow, they already knew the calf was OK, and the loud clicking had changed into a soft, gentle rhythm that almost sounded like a lullaby. It was a familiar song, and Seymour was sure that he had heard it somewhere before. When Ruby spoke to the dolphins with a series of gentle clicks of her tongue, the lullaby stopped. Only the soft splashing of waves on the sand and the sound of the breeze brushing the trees on the ridge prevented total silence. The afternoon sun was low in the sky and night was slowly approaching.

Suddenly a loud groan[61] from Seymour's stomach made Ruby laugh and comment, "Let's go to the food center and feed that beast!" On their way to the food center, Seymour and Ruby checked on the dolphin calf and found Max and Robyn standing by the spa like worried grandparents. Knowing that the calf was in good hands, they moved on to the processor and ordered their favorite meals and drinks. It was a pleasant evening as they ate and discussed the events of the day that had brought them together again. Max entered the food center and asked, "We are returning the baby to her parents. Would you like to join us?"

The happy reunion proceeded with a ritual-like appearance as they proceeded to the beach with dimly lit beacons on each side of the dolphin calf. It was dark outside and the night sky was clear and the stars and moon helped to light the beach. There was a great aura of peace and joy surrounding the small group when the family of dolphins was made whole again. Without speaking, Seymour and Ruby walked slowly to a flat rock near the beach, sat, and stared at the night sky. A warm breeze covered them like a blanket, and they both felt a burning desire to dedicate their being to making the universe better. At that moment, the spirit of the Earth bonded both of their souls and their lives changed forever.

Lightning flashed across the sky, branching into every constellation, but there was no thunder. And, for a moment, the stars were replaced with the face of the Creature.[62] Then everything returned to normal, everything except Seymour and Ruby. It seemed as though the Metatronic™ brains of Max and Robyn could sense the change in Seymour and Ruby, and they both moved to join them on the beach.

Ruby looked at them and asked, "Did you see the Creature in the sky?"

They both answered at exactly the same time, "Yes."

Seymour stared at Robyn and asked, "What does it mean?"

Robyn answered, "Much to do, need to prepare. Everyone meet here tomorrow early."

Meanwhile, Max moved and stood next to Ruby. Seymour turned and took both of Ruby's hands into his. He gently pulled her toward him, and they kissed. It was not just a sign of love but also a seal of the mission to fight the Creature in the days to come. Then Ruby climbed onto Max's back, and, protected by an invisible shield around them, they rose into the night sky and were gone. Seymour walked slowly back to the lab knowing that Robyn would explain to him about what is needed to be done. And the taste of that first kiss still sweetly lingered on his lips.

Later that night, when Max started his descent into Ruby's palace that was high inside Mount Whitney,[63] she opened her eyes and could see the east face of Fisherman's Peak. She knew that she was back home as the strip of bright-purple Sky Pilot flowers blooming just below the summit welcomed her. Max flew through the holographic granite slab on the east cliff that had hidden the palace and gently landed near the main entrance. They had made trips like this many times before, but Max knew that Ruby was different now and there was a great adventure ahead.

Both Ruby and Seymour found it hard to sleep. Although they were located far from each other, staring at the night sky made them feel close. Simultaneously they wondered about why Max called the dolphin calf "the baby"! Max surely new that it was a calf, and he had never made this kind of mislabeling. Then there was the face of the Creature. It made for a very restless night, but sleep finally came, just as Max and Robyn knew it would. They stood watching, and, for the first time, they linked their Metatronic™ brains and shared the events of the day.

Chapter 8
The Creature

The sun had just risen when Ruby and Max returned the next day. Glen had just returned from his latest adventure and met them on the beach. Thunder was booming and lightning flashing from dense clouds overhead when they arrived. Ruby had slept on Max's back during the trip home and back again, but was a little stiff from the journey. After a quick "Good morning" and a high-speed breakfast, Seymour started packing all the gadgets of advanced technology from his hidden home. Meanwhile, Ruby worked with the two robots, Robyn and Max, on the supercomputer and power center of the lab. The faster-than-sound submarine had already been moved to the river under the cave in the island nearby. The storm was not just a coincidence. The Earth was keeping the satellites[64] overhead blinded while the newly formed crew moved everything to the island cave. Everyone knew that the Creature was coming, and that it would be there as soon as the storm was over. Even TB, the tri-blade helicopter, with the help of Ruby's antigravity bricks was busy transporting large parts of the lab to the cave entrance. Each section of the lab was enclosed in a force field to protect it from the storm while it was being moved. Both Robyn and Max used their fusion power sources to keep the supercomputer section powered during the move. Only Glen, the Wicklow Terrier, seemed to be enjoying the work as he would sit and watch in each room. Then there was Devyn, the cat, who was busy chasing those ugly rodents that appeared now and then as the rooms were stripped to the bone exposing their dens. The final task was setting the explosives that would destroy the cave under the lab and leave only a dwelling that appeared to be simple and boring to a technical-minded inspector. The last boom of

56

thunder covered the explosion and the job was done. Everyone moved to the cave in the nearby island except Seymour and Glen. The dog refused to leave Seymour, and the storm was ending quickly. Besides, Seymour somehow felt better with his little scruffy companion at his side and prayed for Glen to be OK when the Creature arrived.

They both went back into the newly formed dwelling. Seymour sat at a simple table with Glen at his side and watched the beach as the storm slowly vanished and a blue sky started to make its appearance in little patches overhead. Then a jet boat appeared out of nowhere and zoomed up onto the beach. A helicopter looking like that of military and three different land vehicles quickly followed. As soon as the beach was secured, a large van drove onto the beach and got parked in a strategic area surrounded by this private militia. Seymour somehow knew that this was the Command Center for the "Regulators Ending Environmental Destruction"

Command Center for REED

REED was a global organization that pretended saving the world and answered to no country's laws. They really used the deception of protecting the environment to control and accumulate wealth. Glen turned, faced the house door, and, for the first time since Seymour could remember, produced an aggressive, low-pitched growl. The house door to the beach blew open, knocking two men wearing body armor to the ground. They quickly rose to their feet and entered the room by pointing their weapons.

Seymour snatched Glen into his arms and shouted, "Don't shoot! We are unarmed!" Others followed into the house as Seymour, with Glen in his arms, was escorted out onto the beach. The area looked like a crime scene, with people in different uniforms and robots searching everywhere. A man in a white coat, holding some sort of scanner, approached them and pointed the object at Glen. Glen softly growled once again, and the scanner sparked and started to release smoke. Instantly, Mr. White Coat dropped his scanner and backed away. This incident forced two robots to turn and approach them. Again, Glen produced a slow, deep growl, and both robots appeared to stop and go to sleep. Then a woman in uniform, who appeared to be in charge walked up and said with an angry look, "What's the problem?"

Woman in charge.

58

Mr. White Coat replied, "There seems to be some type of field in this area that is disrupting our equipment and the robots, Lieutenant."

She replied, "Follow me to the command center. We know that area is safe."

With an escort on each side, Seymour and Glen followed her across the beach with no further problems. The entrance to the command center was really a chamber filled with scanners and electronic sensors. Two robots guarded it with powerful-looking laser weapons. The lieutenant held up a special coded card, and, like an elevator entrance, two thick steel doors slid away from each other to allow passage. She glanced at Seymour and demanded, "Follow me, but leave that animal outside!"

A high-pitched but soft cry from Glen seemed to change her mind and she said, "Alright, but keep him under control."

After they entered the small chamber and the thick steel doors had closed behind them the lieutenant declared, "This will take about five min..." Glen softly growled, the lights went out and the doors into the command center slid open. Someone in the room shouted, "What just happened?" A man in a blue lab coat, sitting behind a monitor panel, shouted back, "The scanners are down and all the electronic devices in the chamber just went dead!" Seymour felt an electronic jolt from Glen to his chest, and a transformation began that would change him for the rest of his life. He heard a faint but familiar rattle sound that he had heard before, but now he knew what it was.

All digital equipment uses ones and zeros that form binary codes. Seymour could now hear that electronic language,[65] understand it, and even control it with his mind. Microprocessors in the robots, hand-held weapons, the master computer, and much more were all under his control. The center of the room held a long rectangular table with three robed individuals wearing white wigs at the far end. The walls on each side of the table held monitors with the faces of at least another dozen witnesses to the room. On the opposite end of the table was a boxed-in chair, slightly lower than normal, so the judges could look down on the person in it. Using his new power from Glen, Seymour mentally ordered a cushion for the chair.

Digital data under Seymour's control.

A robot instantly appeared from the back with a large, red, velvet cushion and placed it on the chair. Seymour walked to the newly made thrown, sat down, and Glen curled up in his lap. Looking slightly downward from his new position, Seymour spoke for the first time, "You came to judge me, so let your trial begin."

The utter chaos that followed was comical. Every monitor in the room was active with questions, commands, and swearing. Technicians were shaking their hand-held instruments and banging on keyboards with puzzled looks. Military guards were looking around with no idea of what they should do next.

Finally the judge at the center of the end of the table banged a gavel and shouted, "Quiet! Quiet!" The room noise slowly diminished, and the man with the gavel shouted, "I am the judge for this...."

Seymour cut in, "Yes, I know. I will call you Mr. J. And the lady on your right is your lawyer. I will call her Mz. L. The man on your left is your technical guide, and I will call him Mr. G. I need no defense lawyer, truth will be my defense. You may proceed."

Extremely annoyed but in a hurry to get this over, Mr. J said "Very well," and turned to Mz. L and said, "Proceed."

Mz. L stared at a small display in front of her and said, "Let's start from the time when you were very young, and you destroyed REED's swamp vine that was developed at great expense from the Venus fly trap.[66] This plant was created to clean the waters in a swamp in Indiana...."

Venus fly trap

Again Seymour interrupted with a loud laugh and said, "Your poison vine was developed to kill endangered species and was being tested in Indiana. You had made deals with leaders in various states to buy the protected lands below value after the animals were removed and then sell them at great profits. Those contracts were signed in advance and appear on all your monitors now. The project was scrapped when you discovered that the animals could learn to escape and I am proud to say I was there to help teach them. Since REED organization is 'global', it needs a G placed in front of its name. I will call you GREED, because it is a better acronym for what you really are."

Chaos again erupted and an elderly man on one of the monitors shouted, "I object!" Seymour raised his hand to produce silence and turned to that monitor, and said, "No, Mr O, since you were the negotiator of the political bribes, you may not object." Then Seymour said, "In fact the contract you made to rebuild the bridge that your factory was destroying in the city is on all monitors now and is the truth." The trial[67] was totally in his control now, so he added, "All your other charges were equally motivated by greed. You set shipping routes so ships could be destroyed for your salvage companies and were short selling stock in the insurance companies to make a double profit on these tragedies. Your orders to the salvage companies are on your personal displays right now—orders to go to places in routes that you had set for commercial ships, but I diverted the ships, and they never sank."

Seymour stopped, took a cup from a robot that seemed to know he needed water, drank a little and placed the cup on the table. The room was so quiet, you could hear the servomotors on the robot as it retreated to the kitchen area. Seymour then turned to another monitor on the wall and said, "I will call you Mz. D since you were in charge of making the very large diamond to cut[68] into enough stones to take over the diamond markets. Again look at your screens to see the sales that were promised but never delivered when the diamond disappeared in a storm."

After another short pause and sip of water, Seymour turned to another face on the wall and stared. Although his expression was blank, there was anger in his eyes. Finally the face declared, "Why are you looking at me? I just write software for maintenance robots."

Then Seymour responded with, "No, Mr. S, you wrote software and sent it to many maintenance robots to shut down generators so the GREED repair division could make huge profits. Lives were lost at hospitals and communities that survived on these energy sources. I almost lost my life trying to repair my unit. You are the worst kind of killer, hiding behind code and software. It's all right there on each of your screens."

A silence took over the command center as all were reading the data displayed on their personal screens. Then Seymour turned to a face on the farthest monitor in the room and declared, "You are the accountant.[69] I will call you Mr. A. You are another killer who hides in the shadows of software and the 'bottom line'. You use your job to justify your evil."

Seymour took a sip of water and turned to face a display of a young woman. "You think you are innocent? I will call you Mz. I. You sell human body parts and tissue from clinics to companies to make lotions and perfumes. When the scandal of your dealings became public, you had to find a new source, so you started hunting baby dolphins. Thus the spear in one of these babies brought you here."

Mr. J slammed his gavel on the table so hard that it made Glen sit up and lean on Seymour's chest. Mr. J shouted, "We are not on trial! You are!"

Seymour put his arms around Glen, stood up, and explained, "Wrong! You have just been through your trial. You are all infected by the Creature known as greed. I have given you the cure—the Truth. How you use it will determine where you will be sent in the end. Use the letters of the names (J, L, G, O, D, S, A, I) I have given you to make two words of four letters each. If you do not change, the solution to the above anagram[70] will be your destiny and you will meet the Creature's master and live out eternity under his rule. You all had good hearts once. Listen to the spirit of the Earth and avoid this terrible end. As Seymour turned the doors of the command center, both opened and he walked onto the beach.

Mr. J was shouting, "Stop him! Shoot him! Kill him!" But nobody moved. Seymour walked across the beach to the pier and onto the small boat. He was only out of view for a few seconds as the boat turned and headed out to sea. Suddenly the command center doors slammed shut, all the electronic equipment came back to life, and robots were back in control. Mr. J screamed "Everyone sink that boat, now!" All the weapons turned, aimed at the vessel, and fired. Over twenty laser beams from hand-held weapons, command center roof, ships in the sea, and tanks on the beach all fired at once. The small boat burst into flames and burned so fast and bright it looked like magicians flash paper.[71] When the laser appeared to go right through Seymour and Glen, they too burst into flames and in seconds all was gone.

Mr. J sat back in his chair and announced, "Now there's a truth I can live with. Let it be recorded that Seymour E. Blox and his dog died at sea." There were some in the center looking down at their displays and wondering. Only one seemed to take Seymour's last words seriously. For the sake of this one, the spirit of Earth had given them all a chance to repent before it was too late.

Truth is often not what we see or hear. Truth is what really happened. When the boat turned and Seymour could not be seen, a portal was opened and Seymour with Glen in his arms dropped down into Mimi, the invisible submarine directly under the small boat. Simultaneously a small electronic device was placed on the deck of the boat that projected a holographic movie of Seymour and Glen on the deck. While the boat was heading for the open sea, Mimi invisibly brought Seymour and Glen to the cave in the nearby island. Everything happened so fast that Seymour with Ruby, Robyn, Max, and Devyn were all watching the burial at sea on a monitor in the cave. Only Glen seemed oblivious to the burial as he played with his favorite toy. Seymour turned and noticed for the first time that Glen's favorite toy was a small ball with all the lands of the Earth on it. It was a miniature globe.

Glen's ball

Anagram Solution

Chapter 9
The Spirit

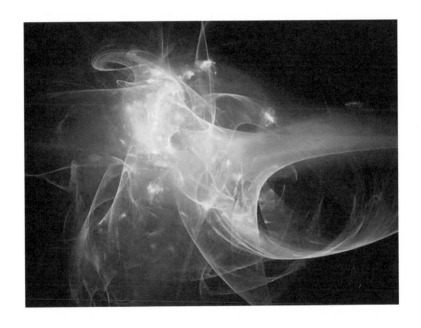

Two days had passed since the raid by REED had forced Seymour and his friends to move into the cave home near his old lab. Ruby was eager to return to her home, but she was afraid to chance the trip for fear of being seen by a satellite controlled by REED. Everyone was busy making the new home in the mountain comfortable. A strong romance between Seymour and Ruby was turning into courtship. Robyn and Max were even getting attached as much as their Metatronic™ brains would allow. Devyn was busy ridding the cave of the undesirable rodents in a manner cats seem to enjoy. Glen, however, had disappeared, and no one knew where he was. He often disappeared for a couple of days so no one was concerned. On the morning of the third day Glen sitting on a large rock at the far end of the cave and barking awakened everyone. He continued to bark until everyone was at the rock. Then before anyone could say anything, he jumped down from the rock and ran right through the cave wall. Ruby went to the wall and tried to touch it, but her hand disappeared into the rock. Seymour put his hand around Ruby's waste and they both walked through the phased array[72]— holographic rock doorway into a long corridor that sloped downward. Glen was nowhere in sight. A force seemed to pull them gently down the path toward a totally dark area. As they walked, the force increased until they were no longer in control and flew into the dark hole. It took only a few seconds to pass through the darkness and float out into another lit passage where Glen stood wagging his tail. They floated gently down in front of Glen and staggered as dizziness prevented total control of their legs. A few minutes later, Robyn and Max joined them and also appeared to be disorientated for a few seconds. Glen woofed as if to say, "Don't wait for Devyn," and proceeded through the passage that was now sloped slightly upward. During the walk Ruby stated, "I think we just passed through some sort of a black hole[73]" Robyn was more concerned with the light that seemed to come from nowhere. Seymour, however, kept his eyes on Glen and pondered how much this small dog had done for him in the past few days.

The passage ended with another rock wall that Glen passed through and went out of sight. They all followed without hesitation as if it was a normal doorway. Ruby grabbed Seymour's arm and shouted "I'm home!" Seymour stared at a beautiful castle inside a mammoth cave. The cave was at least five hundred times larger than the one they just left, and there were gardens and smaller houses around the castle. Ruby was so excited that she ran across the field as fast as she could while pulling Seymour and shouting to people she passed by. It was a small village inside a mountain, and Seymour was awestruck! Robyn and Max followed them like two shadows in the sun. Only Glen noticed Devyn enter the cave with a large dead rat in her mouth. She pranced over to Glen, dropped the rat and licked him on the side of his face. She sat there while her collar blinked and transmitted a message to Robyn that made her stop and look back. Seymour had lost his shadow because Robyn was recording Glen bury something in a small patch of wild garlic[74] that grew near the far wall of the cave. When Ruby reached the palace she shouted to an elderly couple that had come out on a balcony to see why the normally quiet little town was suddenly filled with people shouting. "Mom, Dad, I'm home, and I brought someone with me I want you to meet!" Before her parents could answer, a loud noise came from above.

Ruby's castle

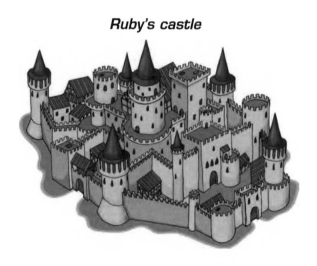

Everyone was shocked to silence by still another unexpected event. A large door in the side of the mountain started to slide open. It had been decades since this door had been used to help build the castle and only a few of the older people even knew it existed. The opening caused panic in many, and they started to scurry for protective shelter. Then TB helicopter[75] flew in and landed in the field behind Seymour. Two passengers disembarked and Seymour recognized them immediately shouting, "Mom! Dad! What is going on?"

"We have no clue," his father said. "This helicopter just landed on our farm in front of the house, and I recognized TB instantly. We were told that you had died in a boating accident, but we knew that if you were alive, then TB would take us to you. So we got in to see if it could. And, my God! It did!"

The large door had closed, and people were starting to come out of their small dwellings as Seymour and his parents hugged and kissed among tears of joy. It took a little while for the chaos to turn to regimented confusion, but everyone eventually gathered in the field and the introductions began.

After a few weeks, everyone knew each other and wedding plans for Seymour and Ruby were well on their way. Many workers were traveling between caves, improving the new base of operation on the other side of the world. Even Seymour and Ruby were using Mimi, the faster-than-sound submarine, to expose corrupt agencies that still plagued the city. Robyn and Max had also made a new friend—a robot named Min that lived with the village's doctor, Paul. Like them, Min also had the plate with the letters GA. Min's Metatronic™ brain instantly bonded with Robyn and Max, and a large amount of history was shared by all three. Most people just knew Paul as 'Doc', but now the GAs knew much more than even Paul knew about himself. Paul was in his late fifties and had accepted Min to be his companion without question when she appeared as a gift over three years ago. When she first spoke, her voice brought him back to when he was young and in love with someone with that same voice. They had traveled to many nations helping the poor and healing the sick. Then she left him to join an organization that was going to eliminate environmental destruction. Paul was devastated and spent years searching for plants that could heal when he stumbled upon this mountain village that needed a doctor.

Paul

As the next few months passed, everyone seemed to have more work than they could handle. A wedding was in the wind and there were many problems in the world that looked like they were created by the Creature and needed Seymour and Ruby's attention. They both also realized that Glen was missing and started to worry. But they took comfort in the saying, "Coincidence? I think not." This came from a book they both read about another dog named Sophie.[76] Somehow they knew that Glen was working on something important.

Ester lived on Jarvis Island[77] located in the South Pacific Ocean. It was an unincorporated territory of the United States until purchased by REED. The island had no ports or harbor and was quickly secured by vessels of REED's military forces. The Center of Jarvis Island had a dried lagoon, where deep guano deposits were mined for about twenty years during the nineteenth century. Because of the island's distance from other large landmasses, its high point is the thirty-sixth most isolated peak in the world.

Jarvis Island

Ester had joined REED many years ago and was now the head of the personnel department with the highest security rating. She lived in an isolated building with no cameras and was considered next in line to be the head of REED. No one questioned how her robot bypassed all her security. The robot simply announced, "Hello. My name is Feeniks, like the mythical bird,[78] but spelled differently. I will be your global assistant. I can translate all known languages for you." Ester assumed that the plate marked GA on the robot stood for global assistant, but it was his voice that shocked her. He had the same voice of a man she loved years ago. She had come to regret leaving him to join REED, especially after seeing the killing of Seymour and his little dog and hearing how a Creature had turned the organization into GREED. She was one of the faces on the wall monitors, and, at one point during the out-of-control trial, she felt the dog's blue eyes staring at her. Then just recently this little dog appeared, and he had the same blue eyes.

Glen's blue eyes

Feeniks instantly commented, "He is a rare breed that can do what is called the 'Glen Sit'."

Ester remarked, "Well, I guess we will just have to call him Glen then." And the dog sat up and wagged his tail.

For the past few months Glen and Feeniks endeared themselves to Ester as she prepared to campaign to be the head of REED. Then one morning, Glen seemed to be all excited as he barked and ran to the door.

Feeniks remarked, "He wants us to follow him," so the three started on a long trek to one of the old abandoned mines near the dried lagoon. Glen ran into a small opening that was left after an apparent collapse of the mine's entrance, and Ester hesitated to follow. Again Feeniks remarked, "It appears to be safe. Let's see what Glen has found."

They both entered into a dimly lit shaft that sloped downward and followed Glen deeper into the mine. Ester was puzzled by the fact that after a thirty-minute walk, the shaft was still dimly lit. Then something seemed to start pulling them off their feet, and they were propelled into an area that was totally dark.

Cave entrance

74

On the other side of the dark area, the shaft was much brighter and sloped upward toward a flat rock wall. Glen was more excited than Ester had ever seen before and he ran right through the stone wall. Without thinking, Feeniks and Ester followed. On the other side of the wall was a beautiful garden with a castle in the distance. Around the castle were small dwellings and everything was inside the largest cave that Ester had ever seen. But the thing that made her heart stop for a second was the man standing and facing her with three robots at his side.

The minute Paul saw that Ester was not wearing a wedding ring, he grabbed her and kissed her. "I never should have let you go!" he said softly. "Now that you are with me again, I will correct that mistake."

Feeniks only took a minute to connect with the other three GAs via Metatronic™ brain telepathy[79] and then remarked, "Hurry, there is not much time."

What happened next was the shortest engagement ever as Min produced a ring box and handed it to Paul while he was standing with his mouth open and staring at Ester. He dropped to one knee and asked "Will you...?"

Ester interrupted and said "Yes!"

Max said, "Hurry! The ceremony has already started. I have the wedding rings. Follow me!"

Robyn had run ahead with Glen to pause the nuptial for long enough to turn the wedding into a dual ceremony and then Robyn placed two more figures on the top of the wedding cake.

In the months that followed, the infection of the Earth by the Creature was being cured. Ester became the head of REED and removed many of the people that were only there to make money. She would take long periods of time off and disappear every now and then. No one seemed to know how or to where. Paul also was seen with a nurse in countries that were being helped by doctors without borders.[80] Corrupt agencies all over the world were being exposed by anonymous sources and computer messages that could not be traced. The forces of good against the Creature were growing and greed in the world was now being exposed. The Creature could not understand the shift toward good and had all his spies working for an answer. His best spy, a large rat named Vile, had disappeared months ago. Even his super buzzards flying high in the sky could not sniff out the remains of Vile if he was dead.

Vile

The Creature had searched every known garlic patch because he knew that was the only place the smell of Vile could be blocked. Nothing on Earth could be found. It was almost as if something underground was working against him.

On a farm in Indiana, in the woods by the Kankakee River, Glen was kneeling with his paws crossed in prayer. It may have looked like the "Glen sit" but this is how he prayed. The bush in front of him glowed with many colors as Glen communicated silently with the spirit. It was not a normal conversation, but more like a video of pictures showing flash backs of how it all started. Flashbacks showing TB that guided Seymour when he was young. Quickly the flashbacks moved to Robyn, who, like the first bird to tell us the earth would soon come back to life, appeared to help Seymour in this rebirth. Ruby's lifetime, the arrival of Max, Paul, and Min were all shown and how they helped in this battle against the Creature. Finally Feeniks, the last robot with a "GA" plate was shown to be like the mythical bird Phoenix that rose from the ashes of REED to help complete the Earth's rebirth.

Mythical bird Phoenix

It had been many years since all this took place and the Earth had changed to a healthy, loving planet to live on. Glen had offspring now that were helping the underground. The GA robot, Max, kept egos in check by limiting everyone's worldly exposure, while Min made sure that enough help was provided to keep the Creature away.

Glen ended his meeting with the spirit and returned to the farmhouse. He knew it was time. He curled up on the porch floor between Seymour's parents and closed his eyes for the last time. But in those final moments, he knew that he had helped Ester's life to be turned back. He knew he had helped move her to the front of REED. He also knew that he had helped take the silent "E" in the title "EARTH ONE" and turn it counter clockwise a quarter turn to make it look like a "W." Glen knew that, like Ester, he had helped move that "W" to the front of the letter group to make the title of this book read true. In his final moments, he knew that he had served his God and by doing so...

EARTH ONE ------> EARTH WON

Epilogue

When Glen went to sleep for the last time, he had a dream. He was exploring a cave that had a bright light in it instead of a dark hole. As his feet left the ground, he could feel the joy and happiness that was in the light. He could hear Sophie calling him. He was sleeping but his feet were moving as he tried to run into the light. Devyn was with him and put her head on his neck to let him know he was not alone. His best friend helped him make that final journey.

The Plot

A young boy walked down to the river,
just to sit and watch the water flow.
As he sat a thought made him quiver,
there was so much he did not know.

A young girl growing up in a big town,
sat on her porch and pondered her life.
As she sat a thought soon came around,
would she find a husband and be a wife?

A good doctor who loved to serve others,
was sad for a doctor he loved went away.
The lady doctor had different druthers,
she wanted to serve in a different way.

The world had become very scientific,
and people used robots to get power.
Destruction of our planet was terrific,
the world was getting cold and sour.

Then four robots came out of nowhere,
to fight back and help save the Earth,
and a dog with blue eyes and short hair,
came and proved to be of great worth.

Satanic creatures tried to get control,
as they corrupted people from within,
but those who had love in their soul,
and a dog, helped the Earth to win.

About the Author

Arthur (Art) F. Seymour—Entrepreneur, inventor, educator, and philosopher:

Art studied electrical engineering at Christian Brothers University and earned his master's degree at IIT. During college, he authored one of the first patent applications on caller ID. He started his career at Motorola and was one of the first engineers to incorporate integrated circuits in color television. He later managed a group of engineers at Zenith Radio Corporation. Art launched E-Blox Inc. after forty-four years of being the President of Elenco Electronics, Inc. At present, he has more than a dozen patents with a few still pending. Greek philosophy is still one of his passions.

Art and Maryann have eleven grandchildren. They both took great joy in telling stories to their grandchildren at bedtime. Art claims that these memories of storytelling, in part, inspired this book. His greatest inspiration in life, however, was his wife Maryann. Maryann went into the light while holding Art's hand on the morning of September 11, 2019.

Maryann, Art's Best Friend

External Links

Robyn[1] from page 2
https://qr1.myeblox.com

Glen[2] from page 2
https://qr2.myeblox.com

astern and on the port side[3] from page 3
https://qr3.myeblox.com

Berkeley Building in Boston[4] from page 4
https://qr4.myeblox.com

Metatronic™ brain[5] from page 4
https://qr5.myeblox.com

laser[6] from page 4
https://qr6.myeblox.com

Hippocampus Abdominalis[7] from page 5
https://qr7.myeblox.com

54.324633, -9.637499[8] from page 5
https://qr8.myeblox.com

Devon Rex[9] from page 5
https://qr9.myeblox.com

Morse Code[10] from page 6
https://qr10.myeblox.com

fusion power source[11] from page 7
https://qr11.myeblox.com

flow chart[12] from page 9
https://qr12.myeblox.com

architects of the city hall[13] from page 9
https://qr13.myeblox.com

mimic octopus[14] from page 12
https://qr14.myeblox.com

cavitator[15] from page 12
https://qr15.myeblox.com

caisson[16] from page 13
https://qr16.myeblox.com

calcium leaching[17] from page 13
https://qr17.myeblox.com

Edward the Confessor[18] from page 14
https://qr18.myeblox.com

GLA[19] from page 15
https://qr19.myeblox.com

climbing tools[20] from page 17
https://qr20.myeblox.com

waterskin[21] from page 17
https://qr21.myeblox.com

pitons[22] from page 17
https://qr22.myeblox.com

microchip[23] from page 18
https://qr23.myeblox.com

Mastodon[24] from page 19
https://qr24.myeblox.com

spelunking[25] from page 19
https://qr25.myeblox.com

Shimeji[26] from page 20
https://qr26.myeblox.com

licorice candy[27] from page 20
https://qr27.myeblox.com

pilea cavernicola[28] from page 20
https://qr28.myeblox.com

T-rex[29] from page 21
https://qr29.myeblox.com

extinction[30] from page 22
https://qr30.myeblox.com

Thomas G Thompson[31] from page 24
https://qr31.myeblox.com

Iceberg[32] from page 25
https://qr32.myeblox.com

welding[33] from page 26
https://qr33.myeblox.com

electromagnetic field[34] from page 27
https://qr34.myeblox.com

Giant Isopod[35] from page 28
https://qr35.myeblox.com

antimatter[36] from page 28
https://qr36.myeblox.com

plateau[37] from page 28
https://qr37.myeblox.com

bayou[38] from page 32
https://qr38.myeblox.com

super-computer[39] from page 32
https://qr39.myeblox.com

bio-copter[40] from page 33
https://qr40.myeblox.com

swamp boat[41] from page 33
https://qr41.myeblox.com

Imperial Stag[42] from page 34
https://qr42.myeblox.com

gas released[43] from page 35
https://qr43.myeblox.com

Full astern[44] from page 35
https://qr44.myeblox.com

triangle[45] from page 37
https://qr45.myeblox.com

telepathy[46] from page 37
https://qr46.myeblox.com

face[47] from page 40
https://qr47.myeblox.com

MCT[48] from page 40
https://qr48.myeblox.com

submersible[49] from page 41
https://qr49.myeblox.com

Bernoulli's Principle[50] from page 41
https://qr50.myeblox.com

interlock torpedo tube[51] from page 43
https://qr51.myeblox.com

industrial robot[52] from page 43
https://qr52.myeblox.com

temper[53] from page 45
https://qr53.myeblox.com

dolphins[54] from page 45
https://qr54.myeblox.com

Delphinus[55] from page 48
https://qr55.myeblox.com

Orion[56] from page 49
https://qr56.myeblox.com

MedTab[57] from page 50
https://qr57.myeblox.com

x-ray[58] from page 50
https://qr58.myeblox.com

AC Current[60] from page 51
https://qr60.myeblox.com

loud groan[61] from page 52
https://qr61.myeblox.com

Creature[62] from page 53
https://qr62.myeblox.com

Mount Whitney[63] from page 53
https://qr63.myeblox.com

satellites[64] from page 56
https://qr64.myeblox.com

language[65] from page 60
https://qr65.myeblox.com

Venus fly trap[66] from page 61
https://qr66.myeblox.com

trial[67] from page 62
https://qr67.myeblox.com

cut[68] from page 63
https://qr68.myeblox.com

accountant[69] from page 63
https://qr69.myeblox.com

anagram[70] from page 64
https://qr70.myeblox.com

flash paper[71] from page 65
https://qr71.myeblox.com

Phased Array[72] from page 68
https://qr72.myeblox.com

Black Hole[73] from page 69
https://qr73.myeblox.com

garlic[74] from page 69
https://qr74.myeblox.com

helicopter[75] from page 70
https://qr75.myeblox.com

Sophie[76] from page 72
https://qr76.myeblox.com

Jarvis Island[77] from page 72
https://qr77.myeblox.com

mythical bird[78] from page 73
https://qr78.myeblox.com

telepathy[79] from page 75
https://qr79.myeblox.com

doctors without borders[80] from page 76
https://qr80.myeblox.com

* Note: An alternative to scanning a QR Code is to enter into any search engine the "http://{address}" shown below the red printing.

There are 80 QR Codes in this book that you can edit and be part of the first SiBoRE™ book written. Not all sites submitted will be accepted. Sites submitted must be judged as better than current site and royalty free to use in a book. This process is believed to be unique and a patent has been applied for.

Submit an edit at: *sibore.myeblox.com*

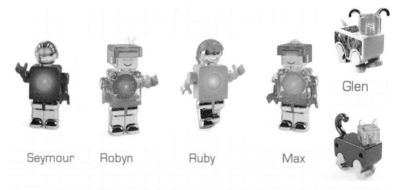

Seymour   Robyn   Ruby   Max   Glen

Devyn

They all light up and stay lit when the power is removed from their feet.
Ask your local toy store for them. Colors may vary.